GHOST SHIP

Published by Disney Press, an imprint of Disney Book Group.

Printed in the United States of America

First Edition
1 3 5 7 9 10 8 6 4 2

Library of Congress Catalog Card Number: 2006909026

ISBN-13: 978-14231-0620-3
ISBN-10: 1-4231-0620-2

DISNEYPIRATES.COM

Ghost Ship

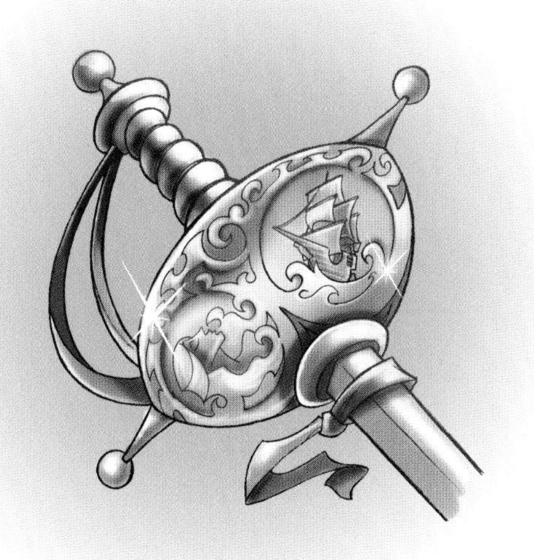

By Jacqueline Ching

Based on characters created for the theatrical motion picture

"Pirates of the Caribbean: The Curse of the Black Pearl"

Screen Story by Ted Elliott & Terry Rossio and Stuart Beattie and Jay Wolpert

Screenplay by Ted Elliott & Terry Rossio

New York

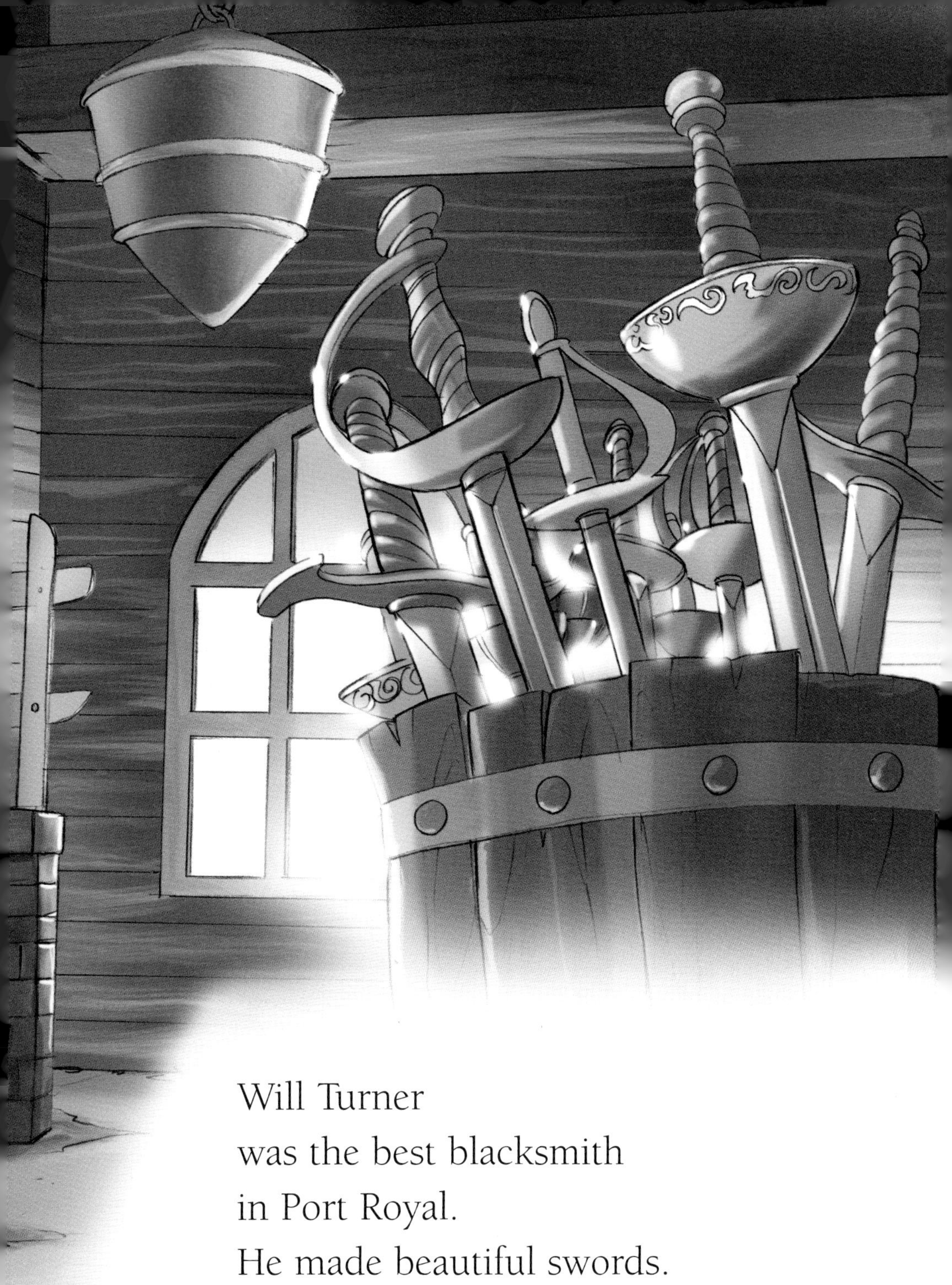

Will Turner
was the best blacksmith
in Port Royal.
He made beautiful swords.

Will taught his friend Elizabeth
how to fight with a sword.
"It is good to know
how to fight with a sword,"
Will said. "You never know
when you might need to use it."

One day, Will and Elizabeth
went to the beach to practice.

Will saw a fisherman
sitting on the shore.
"Why aren't you fishing?"
Will asked him.

The fisherman pointed out to sea.
Will and Elizabeth saw a ship.
"I am afraid of that ship,"
the fisherman said.

"People say it is a ghost ship,"
the fisherman told Will
and Elizabeth.

Will and Elizabeth
went to the harbor.
Suddenly, a ship
smashed into the dock!
"The ghost ship
is causing this trouble!"
the sailors cried.
"The ghost ship
is bringing us bad luck!"

A sailor told Will and Elizabeth
the legend of the ghost ship.

The legend went like this:
The ship first sailed
over one hundred years ago.

The captain of the ship
had a special sword.
The sword's handle had
pictures of the captain's ship
and the captain's true love.

The captain lost the sword
in a battle.

The captain vowed
to get his sword back.
Then his ship sank into the sea.

"Now the captain is a ghost.
His ship haunts the sea,"
the sailor said.
"The ghost captain will not rest
until he finds his sword."

“Will, can you make a sword
like the captain’s sword?”
Elizabeth asked.
“I think so,” Will said.

Will went back
to his blacksmith shop.
He worked all night.

Will hoped that the sword
would be good enough
to fool the ghost captain.

The next night, Will and Elizabeth took the sword in a rowboat. They rowed out to the ghost ship.

They climbed aboard.
The ship was empty
and spooky.

Elizabeth placed the sword
on the wheel of the ship.

Suddenly, the ship came alive!
Will and Elizabeth
were surrounded by ghosts!

The ghost captain saw the sword.
"My sword!" he said.
"At last I have found it!"

Then the ghost captain
saw Will and Elizabeth.
“Run!” Will cried.

Will and Elizabeth ran.
Will jumped into the rowboat.
But the ghost captain
caught Elizabeth!

Elizabeth drew her sword.
She fought the ghost captain.

Then Elizabeth saw her chance.
"Jump!" Will said.
Elizabeth jumped.

The ghost ship sailed away.
"You were right, Will,"
Elizabeth said.
"It is good to know
how to fight with a sword.
You never know
when you might need to use it."